WALT DISNEY'S
Sleeping Beauty

New York Random House

Library of Congress Cataloging in Publication Data

Main entry under title: Walt Disney's Sleeping beauty.

(Disney's wonderful world of reading)

Enraged at not being invited to the princess' christening, the wicked fairy casts a spell that dooms the princess to sleep for one hundred years. [1. Fairy tales] I. Title. II. Title: Sleeping beauty.

PZ8.W188 398.2′1 [E] 73-21794 ISBN 0-394-82798-8 ISBN 0-394-92798-2 (lib. bdg.)

Manufactured in the United States of America.

F G H I J K

0

R

Once upon a time a king and queen
wished and wished for a child.
At last their wish came true.
A princess was born.
The king and queen were very happy.

The queen decided to give a party.
She asked everyone to come.

She even asked the three good fairies.

But there was one fairy who was not asked.
She was a wicked fairy.
When she heard about the party,
her green eyes burned with anger.
"They will be sorry they did not ask me,"
she told her big black bird.

On the day of the party,
all the lords and ladies of the land
came to the castle.

They rode up in fine coaches.
Each coach was filled with gifts
for the little princess.

The party had just begun when
the three good fairies appeared.

"We have very special gifts
for the little princess,"
said the first good fairy.
She waved her wand
over the sleeping baby.
"Little princess," she said.
"I give you the gift of beauty."

Then the second good fairy stepped up.
"Little princess," she said.
"I give you the gift of kindness."

Just as the third good fairy started to speak,
there was a terrible sound.

The castle door flew open.

There — in a cloud of smoke —
stood the wicked fairy.

Her big black bird was with her.

"You did not ask me to your party," she said.

"But I have a gift for the princess, too."

The wicked fairy smiled a terrible smile.
"When the little princess is sixteen,
she will prick her finger on the spindle
of a spinning wheel — AND SHE WILL DIE!"

"Oh, no!" cried the lords and ladies.
"Grab her!" cried the king.

But just as the king's men
reached the wicked fairy—
POOF!—she disappeared
in a puff of smoke.

Then the third good fairy said:
"I still have my gift to give.
I cannot take away the wicked fairy's gift,
but I can change it."
"Little princess," she said.
"You will not die when you prick your finger.
You will only go to sleep. But you will sleep
until a prince comes and breaks the spell."

The king had an idea.

"If there are no spinning wheels," he said, "then the princess cannot prick her finger."

So the king's men burned
all the spinning wheels
in the castle.
They made a great fire
in the yard.

But there was one spinning wheel
that was not burned.

It stood in a little room at the top of the castle.

No one ever went into the room.
No one knew the spinning wheel was there.

Sixteen years went by.

The princess grew up to be very beautiful and very kind. But she was also very curious.

One day she came upon some stairs.
"I wonder where these stairs go,"
said the princess.

She climbed and climbed.
The stairs went around and around —
all the way up to the top of the castle.
There she saw a little door.

So she opened it.

And she stepped into a little room.

There stood the one spinning wheel
that had not been burned.

"I wonder what this is," said the princess.

When she reached out to touch it,
she pricked her finger on the spindle.

Suddenly the princess felt very dizzy.
She lay down on a little bed
and went to sleep.

When the princess went to sleep,
the good fairies came and put
a sleeping spell on the castle.
The king and queen were having dinner.
Everyone went to sleep right where they were.

Even the dogs
and horses
and chickens
fell asleep.
Nothing moved.
Nothing made a sound.

Only a prince
could break the spell.

But the wicked fairy did not give up.
She told her big black bird:
"I will make sure that a prince
does not get into the castle.
That sleeping spell will never end."

She made a great forest of roses
grow up around the castle.
The roses had terrible thorns.
No one dared to go into the forest.
And so the castle slept and slept.

It stayed that way
for a hundred years.

Then, after all those years, a prince rode by.
He saw three women.
They were the three good fairies.

"What is inside this forest?" he asked them.
"No one knows," said the three women.
"No one has ever tried to go in."

"Then I will try," said the prince.

"Take this sword," said the women.

"It is a magic sword."

And before the prince could speak — POOF! — the three women were gone.

The prince cut off one branch with the sword.
Suddenly the branches moved out of his way.
The prince rode into the rose forest.
But he did not see that a big black bird
was watching him.

The bird went off to tell the wicked fairy.
When she heard about the prince,
she flew into a rage.

"I must kill him," she said.
"I shall turn myself into a dragon
and wait for him in the rose forest."

When the prince saw the terrible dragon,
he held up his sword.
The dragon blew hot flames at him.
But the prince was very brave.
He charged the dragon.

The magic sword flashed with light
just before it found its spot.
The dragon screamed
and fell to the ground.
It was dead.

And so the prince rode on.

At last he saw an old castle.

When he went inside the castle,
he saw a strange sight.
No one was moving.
No one was making a sound.

The prince looked around and saw some stairs.
He decided to climb them.
They went up to the top of the castle.
There he saw a little door.

When he opened the door,
he found the sleeping princess.
She was so beautiful
he bent down and kissed her.

Suddenly the princess woke up.
The spell was broken.

When they went downstairs,
everyone was waking up.
  "You have saved us!" said the king.
"Prince, you shall have anything you wish."

"My only wish is to marry the princess," said the prince.

And he did.

The prince and the princess lived happily ever after.